ZOE DISCOVERS THE FEAST OF BOOTHS

ISBN: 9798458247931

Speak to the people of Israel, saying, "On the fifteenth day of this seventh month and for seven days is the Feast of Booths to the Lord. On the first day shall be a holy convocation; you shall not do any ordinary work. For seven days you shall present food offerings to the Lord. On the eighth day you shall hold a holy convocation and present a food offering to the Lord. It is a solemn assembly; you shall not do any ordinary work." -Leviticus 23:34-36

DEDICATION

This book is dedicated to my son, Robert Wallace.

He is tender hearted and caring. He will be a wonderful father one day.

I appreciate his ability to work through problems until he has a solution.

I know God has great plans for him.

God bless you, Robert.

Feast of Booths:

Judaism and Christianity are oriented around two separate liturgical calendars, each rich in its own way but with very little natural overlap between them. Even Jewish and Christian holidays that should overlap (like Passover and Easter) have been decoupled by virtue of the historical self-definition of these two religious traditions.

For Messianic Jews, the biblical holiday of Sukkot offers a wonderful opportunity to reflect upon God's incarnation in Jesus, the Word who became flesh and tabernacled among us (John 1:14). The temporary nature of the booths reminds us not to rely too much on the comfort of material things, and that God meets us in the humble corners of our lives.

As Zoe and her friends enter into the richness of Sukkot, we are also reminded of the Jewish virtue of hachnasat orchim, the welcoming of guests, a special touchstone of this particular holiday. In opening our lives to those around us, we acknowledge that the living water that has been poured into us is meant to be poured out into others. May we, like Zhava and her family, enact this kind of hospitality and in so doing become a link in the chain of Jewish tradition.

Dr. Jennifer M. Rosner

Messianic Jewish author & professor

www.jenrosner.com

A few days after everyone went to the Day of Atonement service, Zhava's dad, Mr. Kaplan, met a truck outside with a small delivery of lumber and metal parts. Zoe and her dad, Mr. Taylor, were just arriving home and walked over to say hello.

Mr. Kaplan said, "Hello there!"

And Mr. Taylor answered "Hi! What do you have here?"

Mr. Kaplan explained, "This is the kit to build our SUKKAH, the booth for the backyard."

"Oh yes!" replied Mr. Taylor, "Is that also called a tabernacle?"

"Yes, it is a temporary dwelling," said Mr. Kaplan.

Zoe asked, "Will you build this all by yourself?"

Mr. Kaplan said, "Well, I was thinking of asking a neighbor I know for some help," as he smiled towards Zoe's dad.

"Can we help, Daddy?" Zoe asked, excited.

"Let's go look at the backyard," said Zoe's dad.

So, they all went to the backyard where Zhava and Mrs. Kaplan were waiting for Mr. Kaplan.

"Hi, Zoe!" cried Zhava, surprised to see her friend.

"Hi! My dad might help your dad build the booth! I hope he says yes!"

While the dads talked, Mrs. Kaplan asked, "Would you girls like some lemonade and cookies?"

"Yes, please!" answered the girls. Then they went inside.

A few minutes later, the dads came in smiling and Zoe had a good feeling. Zoe's dad said to Mr. Kaplan, "Let me help you bring in the supplies and we can start work on it tomorrow morning." Zoe smiled widely at Zhava.

When the dads went outside for the supplies, Jayden and Han were standing at the truck.

Han inquired, "Are you building something, Mr. Kaplan?"

"I am! I am building a booth in the backyard for the Feast of Booths next week!" he answered.

Han said "We are good at building. We built booths at the synagogue the last time we went with you!"

Jayden added, "Do you think we could help you?"

"They would be good helpers, don't you think?" commented Mr. Taylor. Zhava's dad agreed, so the four of them started carrying supplies into the backyard. When Zoe saw them carrying things, she told Zhava, "Come on, let's help!" So the girls went outside to help.

The next day, after breakfast, Zoe and her dad went to Zhava's house to start the project. When they arrived, Jayden and Han were already there. Mr. Kaplan was just explaining when they needed the booth to be done and how they would use it for the eight-day holiday.

Everyone went outside, and Mr. Kaplan and Mr. Taylor started explaining where to put all of the wood and the parts. Jayden and Han were goofing off a little bit, but the dads didn't mind.
Zoe asked, "How long will it take us to build the booth?" And her dad answered, "Just a few hours with all this help, Zoe! Mr. Kaplan has everything he needs."

Inside the house, Mrs. Kaplan was taking out a box of decorations. There were plastic plants and fruits to hang on the sukkah walls and colored paper for making a chain to hang across the front and inside.

Outside, in the grassy part of the yard, Mr. Kaplan laid branches with some leaves still on them. Han asked, "Will we use these branches, Mr. Kaplan?"

Mr. Kaplan said, "Yes, they will go on the roof. The sukkah has only three walls like the models you made in class. The roof needs to have holes in it so we can see the stars at night. We will add the branches and some decorations when we are finished building."

The girls were also helping build when Zhava's mom came out and asked them to come in.

She said, "Girls, can you help me with the decorations?"

Han asked, "Are you making decorations?"

"Yes, Han," Mrs. Kaplan answered. He said, "Can I help you?"

And she answered, "Yes, you can help us!" So, the girls and Han went inside.

Once inside, Zoe, Zhava, and Han started cutting paper strips to create a long paper chain for the sukkah. Each strip was turned into a circle and glued at the end to make a link in the chain. Zhava's mom asked if anyone knew anything about the Feast of Booths. The other children did not know, so Zhava answered. "We live in a temporary house to remember how the Lord took care of us in the wilderness when we left Egypt on our way to the Promised Land." "Thank you Zhava!" said her mom.

"Part of celebrating this holiday is selecting a charity that helps people and supporting that charity with gifts. Who has ideas of people that need our help in the community?" Mrs. Kaplan asked.

"My uncle volunteers at a homeless shelter," said Zoe.

Han offered, "We could go to the park and pick up trash."

Zhava said, "I like to deliver meals to the seniors, Mom."

"Those are excellent ideas," Zhava's mom nodded in approval.

"Now let me show you my favorite part of the holiday," Mrs. Kaplan expressed.

She brought out some small, green branches and a yellow fruit.

"These four items are mentioned together in the Bible. They are called the Four Species. We use them during SUKKOT, the Feast of Booths."

The four items were an ETROG (it looked like a wrinkled lemon), a leaf from a palm tree, three small branches of myrtle and a branch of willow.

"We call this a LULAV. It is a special bouquet used during the prayers!" she explained.

Zoe asked, "Is that what you make your lemonade with?"

Zhava laughed.

"Oh, no!" said Zhava's mom. "We save the special fruit and take good care of it because we use it during the ceremony of blessings."

The dads and Jayden came in and Mr. Kaplan said, "We heard there were snacks in here!" Then, Mrs. Kaplan gave them some drinks and treats.

"Look at our decorations, Daddy!" exclaimed Zoe.

"Those are nice! You three did a good job!" Mr. Taylor answered.

"We are finished," Mr. Kaplan said, "and you are all invited back to the sukkah for lunch after our synagogue service. Is everyone still coming?"

Jayden replied, "Yes!" and everyone else nodded their heads.

Zoe and her dad went home and told Zoe's mom and Zach about building the sukkah and the day of the next service. Mom wrote down the day on her calendar.

Zoe's dad said, "Mr. Kaplan reminded me that the sukkah is a picture of how God protects us and loves us. He dwelt with the Israelites in the wilderness and when Jesus came to be with us here, He dwelt with us in a temporary body until He was raised to be with God."

Zoe's mom proclaimed, "Oh that is a beautiful thought! I can't wait to see the sukkah!"

Everyone went to the Messianic synagogue on the appointed day. The teachers, Marty and Jane, helped the kids finish decorating their little booths with tiny little fruits and colored paper and little, tiny sticks on the roof.

Marty began his story, "In the days of the temple, during the holiday of Sukkot, the people would march around the Temple one time for six days. On the seventh day, they would march around the Temple seven times as a big celebration. There was singing at this big, happy festival too! It's also called the 'Time of Our Rejoicing.' On that last day, the priest would take a container of water and pour it out on the altar as a symbol of the hope for coming rain in Israel, for the crops, and for the people."

Jane added, "But listen to this scripture from Isaiah, chapter 12, verse 3: 'You will receive your salvation with joy like drawing water from a well!' Maybe they were also thinking of the Messiah coming one day."

"That's right, Jane," answered Marty, "and look what happened when Jesus, who is also called Yeshua (which means salvation), was at the Temple during Sukkot:

'The last and most important day of the Feast had come. Jesus stood up and said in a loud voice, "If anyone is thirsty, let him come to me and drink. If a person believes in me, rivers of living water will flow out from his heart. This is what the Scripture says." Some Jews there thought He might be the Messiah, but others said they didn't believe it."

Jane continued, "If you love Jesus with your whole heart, you will do what He wants instead of what you want. The more you practice what Jesus wants, the more you find living water in your life like a spring of joy that never ends! It even gives you extra strength when hard times come."

After the lesson, Marty and Jane prayed with the children for God to bless them. The children said "thank you," took their model booths, and went to meet the grownups.

"Let's go eat lunch in the Sukkah!" said Zhava.

Everyone said, "Hurray!" and ran to meet the parents.

Jayden said, "I know some people that have living water. They are always happy, and they love God so much."

"I know my grandfather had living water. I miss him," whispered Han.

Zhava responded, "I'm sorry about your grandpa, Han."

Zhava looked at Zoe and said, "You have living water, don't you Zoe?" Zoe replied, "Yes! I love Jesus. He helps me feel happy and helps me feel better when I get sad. Thank you for showing me the Fall Holidays, Zhava."

Build your own model Sukkah!

Supplies:
- Small Box, shoebox or a carton
- Leaves from outside and tiny sticks with green on them
- String or Ribbon, Glue
- Markers, Fabric such as canvas or burlap
- Popsicle sticks
- Stickers or pictures from magazines, or drawings
- Craft knife or sharp scissors (for parents to use)

Using scissors, have your parent cut off top of box and one side. You should be left with a floor and three walls with no roof.

Measure the walls and cut fabric or paper to cover the outside and inside walls. There are three walls, inside and out, which is 3 + 3 = 6 walls! So, you need 6 pieces of fabric or paper. You may want the inside and outside walls to have a different look, or they can be the same. Glue paper or fabric to the six walls.

While the glue is drying on the walls, make a cross-section roof with the popsicle sticks. If the roof area is too wide for one stick to cross add a stick to the length, gluing the ends together. Add greenery such as small leaves and tiny sticks with leaves to the top with glue.

For the inside decorations you can make small poster of the seven species in the Bible: wheat, barley, grapes, figs, olives, pomegranates, and dates. I have some cut outs you can copy on the next page. You can also make a tiny paper chain by cutting small strips of paper and gluing the ends to form a chain. The usual decorations for a Sukkah are fruit, vegetables, streamers, posters, and even stars with 6 points, the Jewish star!

If you have any Lego people or other small characters, you can place them in the Sukkah with tables or chairs to celebrate The Feast of Booths!

Have fun! If you want to send me a picture of your Sukkah, I would love to see it. My email address is entertheblessings@gmail.com.

Love, Rene

WHEAT

GRAPES

FIGS

DATES

OLIVES

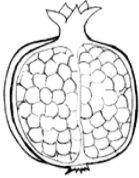

POMEGRANATES

Thank you for joining us on this journey of discovery with Zoe, Zhava, Jayden and Han!

If you and your child (or grandchild) enjoyed this story, PLEASE go to Amazon and post a few lines about what you liked in a review. This will enable more people to experience the joy of the holidays and better understand the Jewish roots of our Christian faith.

Here is your easy checklist:
o Review this book at Amazon.com
o Sign up for free resources, like a FREE guide on how to use this book at EnterTheBlessings.com

May you walk ever closer to God through the Feasts of the Lord.

Recommendations

Do you want to help bring the Gospel of Jesus the Messiah back to his Jewish brothers and sisters? Please consider partnering with my friends, Brian and Liz Crawford of Chosen People Ministries. https://www.chosenpeople.com/site/brian-liz-crawford/

Although we can't visit Israel (as of publication), you can still get the taste, smell and experience of Israel in your own home! Subscribe to ARTZA BOXES! (Cancel anytime, but I don't think you will!) I am an affiliate, which means I will make a little bit of money if you sign up! https://bit.ly/36ZFuZe Use my coupon code ARTZARENEWALLACE for a discount!

Buy gifts and food from Israel: Blessed Buy Israel
Go to www.blessedbuyisrael.com

The enemies of Israel are burning down forests with balloons. Please consider planting a tree. For a $50 donation to our non-profit we will plant a tree and send you a certificate in your name. Go to www.entertheblessings.com (Bless Israel – Plant a Tree)